The Raja
and the Rice
An Indian Tale

First published in 2011
by Wayland

Text copyright © Jillian Powell
Illustration copyright © Elena Almazova
and Vitaly Shvarov

Wayland
338 Euston Road
London NW1 3BH

Wayland Australia
Level 17/207 Kent Street
Sydney, NSW 2000

Series Editor: Louise John
Editor: Katie Woolley
Cover design: Paul Cherrill
Design: D.R.ink
Consultant: Shirley Bickler

A CIP catalogue record for this book is available from the British Library.

ISBN 9780750265379

Printed in China

Wayland is a division of Hachette Children's Books,
an Hachette UK Company

www.hachette.co.uk

The Raja and the Rice
An Indian Tale

Written by Jillian Powell
Illustrated by Elena Almazova
and Vitaly Shvarov

WAYLAND

It was early one morning and
the sun shone brightly on the fields.

"Where is the rain?" asked Tamwar's
mother, looking up at the sky. "If the
rain doesn't come, we will have no
rice harvest."

Tamwar's mother was right. The rain didn't come and there was no harvest.

"We must ask the Raja to give us some rice," Tamwar's uncle said.

So the people went to the palace to ask the Raja, but the Raja refused to help them.

"I'm sorry but I have no rice to spare," he said. "I'm having a rice feast at the palace, and I have asked all my cooks to make something amazing for me."

One by one, the cooks brought
their food to him.

They brought golden balls of rice,
rice cakes, candies...

...and puddings built like palaces.

One by one, the Raja told them to go away.

"These are too ordinary," he
yawned. "I want something
amazing! Something wonderful!"

13

Tamwar washed plates in the palace kitchen to earn money to help his family. He was washing up the plates the cooks had used to make the Raja's feast when, suddenly, he had an idea.

Tamwar got some coloured rice from the palace kitchen and went into the yard.

He used the rice to make a
picture of the Raja on the ground.

When the Raja saw it, he said,
"This is really amazing! Did you
make it?"

"I did, Sir," nodded Tamwar.

"You shall have a reward," the Raja told him. "What would you like?"

"A grain of rice, please," Tamwar said.

The people were angry. They were hungry and the Raja had enough rice for a feast.

"One grain?" the Raja laughed.
"That is a small reward!"

"One grain today and two tomorrow,"
Tamwar said. "Double each day, just
until the rain comes."

"Very well!" the Raja said. "A grain of rice, then double each day until the rain comes!"

Tamwar took the grain of rice home and put it in a pot by the door.

The next day Tamwar had two
grains, then four, then eight...

The days went by and the rain never
came, but the rice kept on coming.
Soon the pot was not big enough!

Tamwar had too much rice for himself and he knew just what to do with it!

"Now it's our turn to have a rice feast!" laughed Tamwar, as he told the people.

As everyone feasted, Tamwar's mother felt a drop of water fall onto her cheek.

Tamwar looked up at the sky. The rain had come at last!

START READING is a series of highly enjoyable books for beginner readers. **The books have been carefully graded to match the Book Bands widely used in schools.** This enables readers to be sure they choose books that match their own reading ability.

Look out for the Band colour on the book in our Start Reading logo.

The Bands are:

	Pink Band 1
	Red Band 2
	Yellow Band 3
	Blue Band 4
	Green Band 5
	Orange Band 6
	Turquoise Band 7
	Purple Band 8
	Gold Band 9

START READING books can be read independently or shared with an adult. They promote the enjoyment of reading through satisfying stories supported by fun illustrations.

Jillian Powell started writing stories when she was four years old. She has written many books for children, including stories about cats, dogs, scarecrows and ghosts.

Elena Almazova and Vitaly Shvarov are an illustrator team from Moscow in Russia. Their favourite stories are those about wizards, wicked stepmothers and magical objects!